"Let's try to hold them off as long as we can!" shrieked Steve.

The blood-maddened great white sharks were charging the boat from opposite directions, churning the water like a ghastly whirlpool of death. The foam was colored a horrifying red! Chris swung one of the oars at the sharks and Steve used the other.

One of the sharks leaped halfway out of the water, ripping away part of the wooden bow. Splinters of wood flew into Steve's face, and he fell back. With each vicious attack, Steve stared into the hideous, empty eyes of the huge shark.

Then, with a tremendous leap, an enraged shark caught Chris's oar in its mouth and snapped it in two like a toothpick!

SHIP OF
TERROR

by Jason Steele

cover illustration by Richard Kriegler

For F.M.B.

Published by Worthington Press
801 94th Avenue North, St. Petersburg, Florida 33702

This edition copyright © 1994 by Worthington Press,
a division of PAGES, Inc.
Original edition © 1991 by Worthington Press

Printed in the United States of America

2 4 6 8 10 9 7 5 3 1

ISBN 0-87406-694-8

CONTENTS

1. The Bermuda Triangle 7

2. Island of Fear 17

3. Is It Really Haunted? 31

4. Red Water 42

5. The Riddle of the Medallion 50

6. Voices in the Night 60

7. Race Against Death 69

8. It's All Over! 79

9. Homeward Bound 90

CHAPTER ONE
The Bermuda Triangle

DEEP evening shadows fell across the large, dimly lit room. Outside, the wind blew. Every now and then, a branch tapped against the windowpane. On a table lay coiled a huge Indian king cobra, looking as if it were about to strike an unsuspecting victim. On a small shelf against another wall, a voodoo doll prepared to do its hideous dance. On one wall, two wickedly sharp Cheyenne tomahawks were crossed, ready for the warpath. And on another, an African witch doctor's mask grinned crazily.

Curled up in a large chair in the middle of the room was fifteen-year-old Steve Ridgley. The light from a single lamp fell on the title of the book he was reading: *Ghostly Legends and Haunted Shipwrecks of the Devil's Triangle.* Steve nervously tugged on his straight black hair and bit his fingernails as he read the book.

Suddenly a sound from outside made him

look up. His eye caught the shadow of a cobra on the floor next to him. For a second, he felt a shiver of fear at the shadow of the deadly snake. Then he shook his head and smiled, chuckling to himself.

The cobra was stuffed, and belonged to his uncle, Paul Mansfield, who owned the travel company Adventure Unlimited. His uncle took tourists on fantastic adventure trips all over the world. Paul had gotten the stuffed cobra on a trip to the Himalayas, the highest mountains in the world. The voodoo doll, the tomahawks, and all the other strange and creepy things in Paul's office were souvenirs, too.

Steve's eyes wandered across the room to a large map of the world that covered most of one wall. In the dim light, he could barely see the different colored pins that were sticking out of the map. Each one marked a place where Adventure Unlimited had gone. Steve and his cousin Chris, Paul's son, had gotten to go on some of the trips.

Steve stretched his legs and settled back into the chair. He returned to the book, a really good, scary book. He was reading it because his uncle Paul was taking a tour group to Bermuda around Halloween to go scuba diving on a shipwreck. The book said that there were a lot of mysterious shipwrecks in the area of the Atlantic Ocean known as the Bermuda Triangle. It said that the sailors who dared to sail across the area called it by another name—*The Devil's Triangle.*

Steve and Chris weren't going on the trip to Bermuda in October. It was during the school year, and they only got to go with Adventure Unlimited during the summer or over school vacations.

Steve looked up from his book. He heard fat raindrops smack against the windows, and then he saw a flash of lightning. He pulled his feet up under him and waited for the clap of thunder. *It's turning into a good night to be reading a creepy book,* he thought.

After he had been reading for about a half hour longer, he began to feel a little sleepy. Steve closed his eyes for a minute. He had been reading a really good part about a tanker in the Devil's Triangle that had heard mysterious sounds on its ship radio and followed the sounds into the Triangle. It was never heard from again.

The only sound in the room was the rain on the roof, mixed with some booming thunderclaps.

Or was it the only sound? At first Steve thought the strange hum he heard was his imagination or something outside. He listened more carefully. No, there it was again, more like a low moaning sound. He rubbed his sleepy eyes and looked around. The sound was definitely coming from inside the room somewhere.

Steve straightened up, listening to the eerie sound. He knew he was alone. Chris and Uncle Paul had gone into town. But who, or what, was making that moaning sound?

Steve didn't want to get up from his chair. Somehow he felt safer there, if there was something or somebody in the room. His eyes darted around the room. The cobra, the tomahawks, the voodoo doll—they were all right where they had been.

Then there was a flash of lightning and he saw it.

The witch doctor's mask that had been hanging on the wall seemed to be moving. Steve stared in shocked disbelief as the hideous mask appeared to float in the air a few inches off the dark wall. He rubbed his eyes and pinched himself to make sure he wasn't dreaming. He gripped the arms of the chair, his panic growing.

No doubt about it, the mask was floating in the air in the dark room, with nothing to hold it up. What kind of strange, unspeakable power did the thing possess to be able to move on its own? As the mask slowly moved toward Steve, he felt a scream rising in his throat. The grisly mouth of the mask, with its rotted teeth, seemed to laugh its horrible laugh. The low moaning got louder and louder until it echoed in his ears. The hideous blank eyes of the mask stared into Steve's, freezing him with fear!

Finally, with a tremendous effort, Steve was able to break the paralyzing hold of the evil mask. He cried out and stumbled from the chair, catching his foot on the table leg and falling to the floor.

"No!" he shrieked, almost feeling the grotesque teeth sinking into the back of his neck.

"Oh, man! I sure wish I had a picture of this!" said a voice—a voice Steve knew well.

"Huh? What's going on?" asked Steve, turning around.

Standing behind the desk, holding the witch doctor's mask on the end of a stick, was his cousin, Chris Mansfield. "Ooooooh," Chris said, making the same moaning sound that had filled the room minutes before. "Admit it, Steve," Chris said. "You were scared."

"I was not," answered Steve, standing up.

"Ah, come on, you were shaking in your boots!"

"I'm telling you, I was not!"

"Oh right, you were just getting up to get a soda and happened to trip. . . . "

"Well," said Steve, "maybe I was a little scared, but only because I was reading this scary book about the Devil's Triangle."

Chris put the mask back on the wall and walked over to Steve. "Hey, let me see the book. That's where Dad's going."

Chris looked nothing like his cousin. Although they were the same age, Chris had blond, wavy hair and blue eyes, and was almost six feet tall. Steve was Vietnamese. Paul's sister and her husband had adopted him when he was three years old. They lived in Columbus, the nearest large city. Steve often visited Chris and Paul in the country. Chris had lived with his dad since his parents' divorce.

Chris took the book from Steve.

"By the way, you jerk," said Steve with a grin. "You'll pay for this. I owe you one and I *will* get my revenge. There's no way you'll escape me."

"Ooh, I'm *so* scared," Chris said sarcastically.

"It's only fair to warn you, that's all."

"So what about this Devil's Triangle?" asked Chris. "Pretty scary stuff, huh?"

"You bet." Steve told Chris some of the spooky legends and strange occurrences he had read about. Chris switched on the lights and they walked over to the big wall map with the pins in it.

Chris studied the Atlantic Ocean and pointed to a spot off the coast of the southeastern United States. "Here it is," he said. "And here's the island of Bermuda. That's where Dad's group will be staying. Dad's old friend Edward will be the group's guide."

"This book says there are hundreds of old shipwrecks in the area," Steve explained. "There are some pretty weird legends. You know, strange sounds and lights, unexplained disasters, lost treasures, hauntings—stuff like that."

"Sounds like you're in the right mood for what I have to tell you," said another voice.

The boys looked around to see a tall, blond-haired man standing in the doorway to the office.

"Hi, Dad. What do you mean? What do you have to tell us?" Chris asked.

Paul sat down in his office chair and put his feet up on the big desk. He stroked his blond beard. "I just got a phone call from Edward in Bermuda. He wants to back out of the trip."

"He does?"

Paul sighed. "I don't understand it," he said.

"It's a perfect trip. The boat's on a shallow reef only a mile from shore. With the legends of ghosts and buried treasure, it would make a great Halloween adventure."

"Why does Edward want to back out?" asked Steve. "I thought it was all arranged."

"Well," Paul said, shaking his head, "he's scared."

Chris and Steve looked at each other.

"He wants me to find another spot to dive," said Paul.

"What's he afraid of?" asked Steve.

"I'm not sure," said Paul. "But I do know Edward doesn't scare easily."

"Did he give any details?" asked Chris.

"Only some story about it being hard to get permits."

"Permits?" asked Steve. "That's all?"

"No," said Paul, shaking his head. "He did mention one other thing."

"What's that?"

Paul looked at the boys. "It's what you were talking about when I came in—ghosts," he said slowly.

"Huh? Ghosts?" exclaimed Steve.

"Edward says there are evil spirits haunting the ship. He was going on and on about tortured screams coming from the ship every night and weird lights around the boat. He

14

says that the lights are the candles of the drowned passengers trapped under the sea."

"Is he serious?" Chris asked.

"I think so," said Paul. "There's some legend about how the drowning passengers lit candles to light the way for the rescue boats. But the boats didn't get there in time to save them and most of them went down with the ship. Or they were picked off by the sharks in the water."

Chris whistled.

"It gets even worse," Paul added. "Every morning, Ed says, the hull of the ship is covered with blood."

"What? Blood? From where?" asked Chris.

Paul shrugged.

"It sounds too weird," said Chris.

Chris and Steve sat quietly for a few minutes, trying to sort out the strange story they had just heard. Could such things actually be true? There had to be an explanation. But what?

Suddenly, Paul jumped up. "It looks like we're going to have to make a trip to Bermuda before I take a tour group there. I'm going to call the airlines," he announced. "Maybe we can get a flight down there to sort everything out."

"What do you mean 'we,' Dad?" asked Chris.

"Well, school doesn't start for another two weeks and I thought you two might like to go, if it's okay with Steve's mom and dad. I could use some help getting this mess straightened out." Paul stood up and walked out of the room to make the call.

"ALL RIGHT!" the boys shouted together, exchanging high-fives.

"Unbelievable! We get to go!" said Chris, jumping up and down with excitement. "Hey, what's wrong?" he asked when he saw his cousin's face. "Aren't you excited?"

"Uh, sure I am," Steve answered slowly. "But there's just one thing."

"What's that?"

Steve held up the book about the legends of the Devil's Triangle. "The stuff that Edward said sounded like the things I've been reading about in this book. You know, the hauntings and ghosts, and horrible legends, and man-eating sharks, and awful things like that."

"What about them?" Chris asked.

"Well," replied Steve quietly, with a strange look on his face. "What if they're true?"

CHAPTER TWO
Island of Fear

CHRIS leaned past Steve's shoulder to peer out the small plane's oval window. Far below, the boys could make out specks of land rising out of the water. Chris pointed toward the islands.

"There's Bermuda," he said.

The plane circled above the main island. It swayed to the right and touched down with a jolt on the runway. Green hills rose beyond the airport's main terminal. Slender palm trees towered over the small houses and stood out against the sky. The bright colors of the tropical flowers almost hurt their eyes.

"Let's try to catch a taxi," said Paul. They were making their way through the crowded airport's small lobby. A dented, yellow Mercedes with rusting fenders was parked at the curb outside. An old man with short, frizzy gray hair and skin the color of milk chocolate was sitting in the driver's seat.

"Can you take us to Somer's Wharf?" asked Paul.

"Sure," he said. "I'll take you there for only 10 dollars."

"Okay," Paul said as he slid into the seat next to the driver. Chris and Steve piled into the backseat. The old man stowed their duffel bags and backpacks in the trunk.

"Come down on vacation?" asked the old man, slipping behind the wheel. With a lurch the car pulled quickly away from the curb.

"Scuba diving," said Steve.

The driver looked over at Paul with a quick glance.

"We're interested in seeing a shipwreck off the island of St. David's—the *Brittania*." said Paul.

The old man took his eyes off the road to look at Paul. His jolly face turned stony for a second.

"You stay away from that wreck," he said, "There are very bad folks down there, evil people," said the driver, lowering his voice to almost a whisper, even though no one else could hear him. The boys could see in the rearview mirror that the driver's eyes had taken on a frightened look.

Chris glanced at his cousin and shrugged his shoulders.

"The ones who drowned in the wreck," the driver continued. "Their spirits haunt the ship!"

"How do you know the ship is haunted?" asked Steve.

"The Devil himself haunts that ship," said the old man, his eyes back on the road ahead. "You stay away from it, you hear?"

"Do you know anything about the sharks?" asked Chris. "Or the strange lights that flicker at night?"

"Or the blood?" asked Paul.

But the driver said nothing for the rest of the trip. It was as if he hadn't heard their questions. The boys knew that only one thing would make a person act like that—terror. Bringing up the subject of the wrecked ship had closed the driver's mouth with fear!

Ahead, on a small bluff overlooking the beach, Chris spotted a small village. The old man pulled the car up to a house at the edge of the village. A sandy path led from the road to the house. Next to the house was a little shop. In front of the shop was an old, sun-bleached sign with faded letters that said Edward's Scuba Diving School.

The old man got out of the car and took the bags out of the trunk. Paul paid him. "You remember what I told you," the driver said, getting back into the car and leaning out the window. "Stay away from that wreck."

The engine sputtered and the car sped away. Paul led the boys down a narrow path toward the house. A wide porch was open to the sea. Near the porch railing stood a slim, balding, dark-skinned man in his late forties. He was wearing ragged blue cut-offs and a pale pink T-shirt.

The man was gazing out at the beach, where waves washed onto shore. He seemed lost in his thoughts and didn't seem aware of the visitors as they followed the path to the house.

"Edward?" called Paul, as they neared the house.

The sound of Paul's voice startled the man.

"Paul?" The man looked shocked. "W-what are you doing here?"

"I just came down to see how my old buddy was doing," said Paul. "You sounded a little shaken up when I talked to you on the phone the other day."

"I'm doing okay," Edward said, his eyes shifting from Paul to the two boys. Then, lowering his voice, he said, "Look, man, I warned you about coming down here. You must be crazy! It's not safe."

"Come on, Edward," Paul answered with a smile. "We've gone on enough adventures together for you to know that a little danger never frightened me," said Paul.

"It's different down here, man," said Edward, shaking his head. "You don't understand. You shouldn't be here. And bringing the kids—it's insane!"

Just then a woman came to the door. "Is someone here, Edward?" she called.

"It's Paul Mansfield, from Ohio," he answered.

"Paul?" said the woman, opening the screen door. "I didn't expect to see you."

"Nice to see you again," said Paul. Edward introduced Marguerite, his wife, to the boys.

"How about something cold to drink?" asked Marguerite. Chris and Steve nodded and watched as she slipped back inside to get the drinks.

"I thought I explained everything to you over the phone," said Edward, keeping his voice low. He was wringing his hands as he talked.

"You didn't explain everything," said Paul, looking directly at Edward. "It just doesn't add up. I've got a feeling there's something you're not telling me."

"Like what?" Edward asked, looking away.

"How should I know?" asked Paul. "Look, we've known each other for at least 10 years. I know you well enough to tell when there's something on your mind. Why won't you help me get the *Brittania* ready for our customers by the end of October?"

"I can show you plenty of ships," said Edward, getting up to walk to the edge of the porch. "Only stay away from the *Brittania*."

"No other ship will do," said Paul, following Edward. "It's the only wreck close enough to shore, within easy reach of inexperienced divers. Besides, you know the legends about it, the ghosts and all. It's perfect for a Halloween adventure."

"And *you* know the legends about the Bermuda Triangle. I'm not going to tell you again," said Edward, turning around to face Paul and the boys. "If you want to stay friends with me, you'd better find another ship." His voice was hard and cold, and his eyes were steely. "Or else find another guide."

The boys stared at Edward. The fear in his face was unmistakable. They hardly recognized him as the same man. Just then, Marguerite returned, carrying a pitcher of orange juice and five glasses on a small tray.

"Is everything all right?" she asked, setting the tray down on the table in front of her husband and sitting down next to him.

"Everything's fine," said Edward tightly, passing a glass to Steve.

"I came down to try to convince Edward to help me on the *Brittania*," said Paul.

Marguerite looked at her husband, her eyes

darting nervously from him to Paul. At the mention of the haunted ship, she pressed her hands together in her lap and nervously wrung them together.

"Coming down here won't change a thing," said Edward. "All the money in the world wouldn't get me on that ship!"

"But why?" pleaded Paul.

"I'm warning you," he said. "Diving from that wreck will only bring trouble—terrible trouble."

"What kind of trouble?" asked Paul. "You're not making sense, Edward."

Marguerite touched her husband's arm. "Maybe you should te—"

"Silence, woman!" shouted Edward, banging his fist on the table so hard that several glasses shook and clanked together.

Marguerite ran into the house sobbing.

"She's not feeling well," Edward said softly. He set his glass on the table and leaned forward with his elbows resting on his knees. He took a deep breath. "Look, what if I told you that all the legends are true? What if I told you the wreck really is haunted?"

Steve looked at Chris with wide eyes. "H-how do you know it's haunted?" Steve asked, turning to Edward.

"At night, you can see eerie, yellow lights

on the wreck," said Edward. "If you watch the lights long enough, they start to move."

"No way!" cried Chris.

"It's true," said Edward.

"How do you know?" asked Paul.

Edward paused, gazing out to sea. Then looking back, he leveled his gaze at Paul and answered, "I've seen them."

Steve gasped. "Y-you've seen the lights?"

"But that's not all," Edward said, drumming his fingers nervously on the table. "You can hear screams at night, too, hideous screams, that make your hair stand on end. They're the screams of the drowned men and women. And the banging noises, the distress signals. Everyone in the village knows it's the ghost of the captain, trapped in his cabin. He was trying to signal for help when he went down with the ship."

Edward took a drink from his glass. Chris and Steve noticed his hand was shaking as he tried to drink.

"It's hard to believe," said Chris.

"Yes, but it's all true," said Edward. "Did I tell you about the blood washing up against the sides of the ship?"

"Yeah," said Paul.

"People say it's the blood of the missing divers," said Edward.

"Missing divers?" asked Paul. "What do you mean?"

"Two divers disappeared last week while exploring the wreck," said Edward. "Some people in the village say that the sharks ate them. Others say the ghosts got them. Take your pick."

Edward's words died away. The boys and the men were quiet.

"But don't take my word for it," said Edward finally. "Come and see for yourselves."

He stood up quickly and walked off the porch. Paul looked at the boys and nodded. Then he followed Edward down the path to the dusty road.

"What do you think is going on?" asked Chris when they were alone.

"I don't know," answered Steve, shaking his head. "But I know one thing. Edward and Marguerite are really scared of something."

"You know it! Do you really think it could be ghosts?"

"Well," Steve said, "we've seen some pretty strange things on the trips we've taken. Do you think that really was the Loch Ness monster that we took a picture of in Scotland?"

Chris rubbed his chin, thinking back on their recent trip to the Scottish highlands and the legendary lake. "I don't know," he sighed.

"Before we went I didn't think it really existed. But actually seeing something out there made it seem real."

"Hey, come on, let's catch up!"

By the time Chris and Steve caught up with the two men, they were already walking along a narrow path toward the village. Paul was a few strides behind Edward, who was walking fast.

The streets of the village were crowded. It took almost 15 minutes for them to pass through town to the beach. Near some large rocks at the end of the beach, a rickety wooden pier jutted into the bay. Several wooden rowboats were pulled up onto the beach. Edward kneeled down in front of one of the rowboats.

"Look at this," he said. He pointed to a row of deep, jagged scars on the side of the boat. At one end of the boat, a hole several feet wide had been ripped open.

"They look like teeth marks," said Chris.

"That's right," said Edward. "This was the boat of the missing divers. Those are from the teeth of man-eating great white sharks."

The boys gasped. Steve nudged Chris and nodded toward the back of the boat. "What do you think that is?" asked Steve.

Chris noticed the dark red stain that spread

over the rear seat and onto the floor of the boat. "I think it's blood," he answered grimly.

"Have you seen these sharks?" asked Paul.

"Sure," said Edward.

He stood up, reached into his pocket, and pulled out a small, brass medallion, about the size of a large coin.

"See this?"

The metal glittered in the bright sunlight. Engraved in thick, straight letters was the name of the haunted wreck, *Brittania*.

"Did it come from the ship?" asked Steve.

"That's right," said Edward. "I saved it from the engine room of the *Brittania* once a long time ago when I was diving out there. It's my good luck charm. I never go anywhere without it—never. Without this good luck piece, I'd never have gotten away from the sharks myself."

The boys looked at the huge chunk that was missing from the back of the rowboat as Edward spoke. The wood was splintered and ripped.

"As long as you have your good luck charm to protect you," asked Paul, "why can't you take us out to look at the ship?"

"You weren't listening to me," said Edward softly, but with tension in his voice. "I told you this protects me from sharks."

"So?"

"I never said it could protect me from evil spirits. Or protect you either. Or the boys," he added, looking strangely at Chris and Steve.

"I still think you're trying to hide something," Paul said.

"Hide? I've got nothing to hide," Edward cried angrily. "I'm only trying to save you from that!" he said, pointing at the rowboat. "Or worse! Look, why not let me show you another ship? There's one on the other side of the island. Your customers will never know the difference."

"Let's talk about it later," said Paul, trying to calm his friend. "Let's go back to the house. We need to get our things and go to Marlow's Boarding House."

Silently, Edward led the way through the village. When they returned, Marguerite was sitting on the porch staring out to sea with the same odd expression that the boys had seen on Edward's face earlier. She didn't notice them until they were coming up the steps. She was startled when she heard them.

"Sorry," said Paul. "We didn't mean to frighten you."

She looked at Paul and answered, "It wasn't you who frightened me." Then she got up and went inside without another word. Paul and Edward both stared after her.

"Say hello to your son for me," said Paul to Edward. "He must be be about nine or ten now, right?"

At the mention of his son, Edward whirled around and faced Paul. "W-what?" he muttered, with a strange, almost frightened expression on his face. "Oh, uh, yes, he's nine. He's . . . he's camping with some friends on another island."

Paul stared hard at Edward. Then he said, "Let me know if you change your mind about the tour. And say good-bye to Marguerite for us."

Edward's face softened a little bit. His eyes looked sad. "She's not herself," he said. "She's had a lot to think about lately."

Paul put his hand on his old friend's shoulder. "I know something's on your mind, old buddy. I hope you know you can talk to me about it anytime."

For a second, Chris and Steve thought that Edward might be ready to talk. But then his face grew hard again, and his eyes narrowed.

"There's nothing to talk about, Paul," he said.

Paul looked at him for one last time and said, "Well, you know where to find us."

"I know," Edward answered.

As they started to leave, Steve and Chris

waved back to Edward. But he only stared at them.

Paul said nothing as they walked to their hotel. "How long have you known Edward, Uncle Paul?" Steve asked.

Paul didn't answer.

"Uh, Dad? Steve asked you a question."

"Huh?"

Steve repeated his question.

"I've known him for about 10 years."

"What's wrong, Dad?" Chris asked.

"I'm still thinking about Edward and his wife," Paul said, looking out at the sea.

"What do you think's bothering him?"

"I don't know," said Paul, glancing at the boys before climbing the stairs to the little hotel's lobby. "I wish I knew if he was telling the truth, about the sharks, the ghosts . . . everything."

"Well, we saw the blood in the bottom of the boat."

"Yeah, I know," Paul answered, pulling on his blond beard. "But I have a feeling there's more to it than that—maybe a whole lot more."

CHAPTER THREE
Is It Really Haunted?

BRIGHT sunlight streamed into the boarding house breakfast room the next morning. It fell on a letter addressed to Chris and Steve. Chris ripped open the envelope as they sat down at their table.

He read it quickly. "Dad's gone to another island. He's looking for another guide who might take him out to the wreck. He says we can go swimming or fishing, or just mess around. But we have to stay out of trouble."

"He always says that," said Steve with a grin. "Why does he think we're going to get in trouble?"

"I don't know," answered Chris. "Maybe it's because we got kidnapped on our trip to Scotland, or because I broke my leg hang-gliding in California, or because you got lost in that rain forest in Brazil!"

Both boys laughed loudly and exchanged a

high-five. "Maybe your dad's right," Steve said. "Let's try not to get eaten by a shark today."

"Or captured by a ghost."

Just then the door to the kitchen opened and out came Mrs. Marlow, the old, white-haired woman who owned the hotel. She served them johnnycakes, onions, and eggs, strawberries, and milk.

"What are you boys planning to do today?" she asked.

"Fish," said Chris, shoveling the eggs and onions into his mouth.

"Ah, well then, bring us home a nice, sweet rockfish, why don't you," she said.

"We'll try," the boys promised.

After breakfast, Chris and Steve followed the trail along the beach to Somer's Wharf. Leaning against the open doorway of one of the shops was a short, heavy man with a thick, black beard.

"Come to rent a boat?" asked the man.

"Yes, sir," said Chris. "And some fishing gear."

Chris chose two fishing rods from the wall outside the shop. Steve filled a plastic bag with bait from a tub.

"Are the rumors true about sharks?" asked Chris.

"They're not rumors," said the man, holding out his badly scarred arms. "No rumor could do this to a man's arms."

The boys stared at the hideous, fiery red scars. Then they noticed the man was missing two fingers on his left hand. Chris dropped some money into the stump of a hand.

"Your boat's at the end of the pier," said the man. "Be careful."

Walking out to the boat, Steve asked, "Do you think it's all right to go out in this boat? I mean, did you see that guy's hand and arms?"

"Sure I saw them," said Chris. "I think it'll be okay if we're careful. They wouldn't rent boats if it was really dangerous. Let's just keep an eye out for sharks."

"Well, I still don't feel that good about going out there in a little boat."

Chris poked his cousin on the arm. "Hey, no problem if you don't want to go," he teased, "you can stay at the hotel and help Mrs. Marlow make the beds. That doesn't sound too dangerous."

"I never said I didn't want to go," Steve answered with irritation. "So knock it off!"

They called a truce and found the 12-foot wooden dinghy tied to the dock. It had a small motor and a pair of oars. Steve stepped into the boat and Chris passed the fishing gear to him.

"Where to, Captain?" Steve asked as Chris climbed in.

"That guy said the fishing's good along the outer reefs, past Smith's Island."

"Do we have enough gas?"

Chris checked the gauge. "We've got a full tank," he said. "And we always have the oars, if *you* want to row!"

"No thanks. We're on vacation, remember?"

Chris started the engine up and soon they were skimming over the blue water toward Gate's Bay. The small shacks by the docks and the village houses grew smaller. Leaving the shelter of the bay, they rowed into a stiff breeze. Steve sat in the front of the boat, the spray splashing against his face, while Chris steered.

"I think this is the good fishing place," shouted Chris, cutting the engine.

As the boat rocked gently back and forth in the warm sun, they baited their hooks and lowered their lines into the water. Far away, they could hear the sound of fishing boats making their way back to the harbor.

"This is the life," said Chris with a sigh, leaning his elbow against the side of the boat.

"Except for the little matter of the great white sharks," answered Steve.

"Come on, what's a little shark?"

"I think you're about to find out. Look out! Behind you!" Steve screamed.

Chris jumped back from the edge of the

boat, causing it to rock and tip. "Where?!"

But Steve was laughing hysterically. "Paybacks!" he screamed. "That's for scaring me with that witch doctor's mask back home! You should have seen your face, Mr. Tough Guy! *What's a little shark?*" he added, imitating his cousin.

"Okay, okay, I get your point," Chris muttered.

They fished for a few hours, without any luck. But they didn't really care. By then they were both hungry, and Steve rummaged through his backpack for the lunch that Mrs. Marlow had fixed for them.

"I think I could get really tired of these things," Steve said, passing the johnnycakes to Chris.

"You and me both," answered Chris.

After lunch, they rowed further away from the shore looking for a better fishing place. They spent the rest of the afternoon drifting and watching their fishing lines in the water.

"Not even a nibble," said Chris, shaking his head. "It looks like Mrs. Marlow won't get her nice, sweet rockfish, whatever that is."

"Ready to turn back?"

"I guess so. Hey, where are we?" asked Chris, looking at the coastline for the fishing village. "I think we drifted a long way."

The Gulf Stream's strong current had carried

the boat down the coast toward a deserted part of the island.

Steve scanned the shore. "I don't see the village anymore. But what's that over there? Near that little island."

Ahead of them, about a mile offshore, a dark shape rose mysteriously out of the water. Chris squinted to see better. "Beats me," he said. "Let's get a little closer."

Chris reeled in his line and placed the oars into the metal locks on each side of the boat. He pulled on the oars and the boat moved forward.

After several minutes of rowing he said, "It's a lot easier moving this boat with the engine."

"Take it easy," said Steve. "We're almost there."

They were less than 300 yards away from the shape. "It looks like the hull of an old ship," said Steve. "I think I can just make out some letters on the ship's bow."

"What's it say? You have better eyes."

"Brittania," he said excitedly.

"Brittania!" cried Chris. "Are you sure? You mean that's it? That's the haunted ship?"

Steve said nothing.

"Let's go in closer," said Chris, pulling at the oars again.

Steve put his hand on the oars. "No, wait

a minute," he said. "I think we're close enough."

Chris stopped rowing and they stared at the ship from less than 50 yards away.

"From here it just looks like an ordinary wreck," Steve said.

"I can't see why Edward's so afraid of it," said Chris. "He said there was blood on the hull. But I can't see anything from here."

"Okay, let's get closer," said Steve, hunching forward in the boat. "But take it easy. Go really slow and be quiet."

Chris rowed the dinghy closer. The *Brittania* lay tilted on its side. It looked large, even though only a quarter of its hull rose out of the water. The rest of the boat was under water.

The boys remembered what Paul had told them about the wreck. It was a luxury cruise ship that had struck a reef in a terrible storm one night about 80 years ago. Half the 200 passengers had managed to make it safely to shore. But the rest, along with the captain and most of the crew, had been trapped below the deck and died there.

"It's awesome," Chris whispered. "Just like the *Titanic!* Think about all those people going down."

Steve tried to clear his head of the sound of screaming that must have filled the air on that fateful night. "Over a hundred people, it's terrible to think about. And they weren't the only thing in the water that night."

"What do you mean?" asked Chris.

"Think about it. If there are sharks now, there were sharks then."

Chris whistled low and fell silent. They gazed at the hull for several minutes, imagining the terror of that stormy night so long ago.

Chris started to row the boat up to the *Brittania's* rusting hull.

"Look!" he whispered sharply. "There's the blood," They stared in horror at the deep red water along the waterline of the hull.

"There could be sharks anywhere around us now," Steve whispered. "There's so much blood, they must have just killed something here."

They were within 15 yards of the hull. Chris carefully and slowly rowed around the part of the hull sticking out of the water. They could see railings, portholes, and ropes. They could also see dark shadows gliding in and out of holes in the wreck under the water. But, in contrast to the night of the wreck, when the horrendous and pitiful screams of the dying must have filled the air, the only sound was the gentle lapping of the waves against the rusting hull.

Chris had rowed almost all the way around the exposed part of the wreck when he suddenly stopped rowing. "Did you hear that?" he asked.

"Hear what?"

"I don't know," Chris answered. "It sounded like hissing or buzzing or something."

Steve listened carefully. "I didn't hear anything."

"I'm going to go a little closer."

"Be careful!"

"Listen! There it is again," whispered Chris.

Steve nodded. This time he heard it, too. "Voices!" he whispered, pointing to an open porthole in a part of the ship that was just above the waterline. "Y-you don't think it could be . . . ghosts, do you?"

"I—I don't know," Chris answered. "It's impossible, but—"

"Shhh!" Steve said.

One voice shouted something.

"It's Spanish!" said Steve.

There were several voices inside the ship speaking Spanish. The one doing most of the talking had a hoarse, raspy wheeze, as if he had trouble breathing.

"Can you make out anything they're saying?" asked Chris.

"No way," said Steve, shaking his head. "They're talking too fast."

"What good is taking Spanish in school if you can't understand it?" asked Chris.

Steve gave him a dirty look.

They both listened to the voices, all the time keeping watch for sharks.

"That guy with the wheeze sounds mad," said Chris.

"There's something familiar about one of those voices," Steve said after they had listened for a while. "I can't think where I've heard it before, but I know I have."

Just then their boat was lifted toward the side of the ship. For one terrifying second, each boy thought it might be a shark pushing against the dinghy. Their hearts were in their throats. But the water was clear and they realized it was only a wave.

Then another, bigger wave pushed the boat toward the *Britannia*. It struck the hull with a loud crash. The voices inside the ship became quiet.

"Start the engine! Let's get out of here!" Steve whispered hoarsely.

Chris pulled frantically at the rope, but the engine wouldn't start. They heard a metal door slam somewhere inside the ship, and then the sound of feet running up stairs echoed through the wreck. They heard the voices again, louder and closer.

"Hurry up," cried Steve. "They're coming!"

"I'm pulling as fast as I can," Chris answered. He tugged at the rope until his hands were raw. After what seemed like an eternity, the engine coughed and sputtered to life.

"Head for that little island," shouted Steve above the engine's noise. "We might be able to get behind it before they come out of the wreck."

With the motor whining and straining, Chris steered full speed toward the island. Steve kept his eyes on the ship, watching for the men to emerge on the deck.

"Still no sign of them!" he shouted. "Hurry! Can't this thing go any faster?"

Waves slapped against the dinghy as it raced over the waves. Then suddenly, he saw a head appear on the deck of the ship.

"Chris! There's one of them! We're dead!" he screamed.

"No, we're not," Chris answered calmly.

Steve looked around and saw that they had entered a sheltered cove on the tiny island. They were out of sight of the men on the wreck. The engine stopped and they glided to a stop in the cove.

"Whew, that was close," said Steve as he collapsed against the side of the dinghy.

"I've got some good news and some bad news for you," said Chris. "The good news is we're hidden from those men."

"What's the bad news?"

"I didn't shut the motor off. We're out of gas."

CHAPTER FOUR
Red Water

"OWW, my aching arms!" moaned Steve after they had rowed to shore hours later. Somer's Wharf was deserted when they returned the dinghy. The boat rental shop was locked, the windows dark. They tied the boat to the dock, and started back to Mrs. Marlow's, threading their way through the streets of the village.

"Whose voices do you think we heard?" whispered Chris.

"I don't know, but I don't think they were ghosts," said Steve. "I think there were at least three or four guys."

"Do you remember where you heard the one guy's voice before?"

"No," answered Steve, "and it's driving me bonkers."

"Look, there's a light on in the hotel lobby," said Chris. They ran up the porch steps and burst into the hotel. They found Paul worriedly pacing the floor in the lounge.

"Where have you two been?" he cried, rushing toward them.

"Dad! We—"

"Now, now, don't get excited," said Mrs. Marlowe, marching out of the kitchen. "Didn't I tell you they'd be all right?"

"We saw the *Brittania*," said Chris, slumping into a chair.

"What were you doing near the *Brittania?*" Paul asked sternly. "I think you'd better tell me the whole story."

The boys took turns explaining everything they had heard and seen. When they were finished, Paul just sat in his chair, frowning.

"I don't like it," Paul said, pulling on his beard like he always did when he was thinking. "Suppose we all go back out there tomorrow and have a look around? That's the only way to get to the bottom of this."

Later that night, as the boys were getting ready for bed in their room, Steve was standing by the window. He was gazing out at the sky and the sea when he suddenly said, "That's it!"

"What's it?" asked Chris.

"That voice I heard out on the wreck this afternoon, the one I thought I recognized."

"What about it?"

"I figured out whose voice it sounds like," answered Steve.

"Yeah? Whose?" Chris asked.

Steve gave his cousin an odd look. "Edward's," he said.

"But that's crazy! Why would Edward be on the boat? He says he's scared to death of it. He said all the money in the world wouldn't get him out there."

Steve shook his head. "I know its sounds weird," he said. "And maybe I'm wrong. But there was just something about the voice that made me think it was Edward on that wreck."

"But all the guys were speaking Spanish."

"Well, let's tell your dad about it anyway," Steve answered. "Maybe he knows if Edward can speak Spanish."

*　*　*　*　*

In the morning after breakfast, Chris and Steve took Paul to the shop where they had rented the dinghy. The same fat man with the beard was standing behind the counter.

"Come in late last night, eh?" he asked.

"Ran out of gas," said Steve.

"It happens," said the man.

"I'd like to rent the dinghy again," said Paul.

He paid the man and they walked out to the end of the dock. The dinghy was where they had left it the night before.

"Uncle Paul, do you know if Edward speaks Spanish?" asked Steve as they pulled away from the dock.

"No, I don't know. Why?"

Steve explained about hearing the voice that sounded like Edward's.

"You think he was one of the men on the wreck? That's impossible!" Paul said.

"That's what we thought, Dad," added Chris. "But Steve's pretty sure that he heard Edward's voice. We have to find out."

Paul shook his head. "If it's true, why on earth would he be out there?" Then he fell silent.

They made their way out to the old wreck, following the same route they had taken the day before. After a while, Chris squinted into the bright sunlight and called out, "There it is."

They cut the engine and rowed, edging slowly closer. Steve was trailing his hand in the clear blue water as they approached within a few yards of the wreck.

"Arrggh!" he cried when he pulled his hand from the water. "My hand! It's all red!"

"There's blood in the water!" Paul said, looking around. "Where did it come from?"

"From the missing divers?" asked Chris.

"Even if 20 divers had drowned," said Paul, "there wouldn't be this much blood."

Steve was washing his hand off, splashing it in some clearer water. Suddenly Paul cried, "Steve! Stop splashing your hand around like that! A shark might think it's something to attack!"

Paul lunged for Steve and pulled him back from the edge of the rowboat. At the same instant, they felt a heavy thud on the bottom of the boat, and then another. There was a flash of something white passing under the rowboat at great speed.

"Look out!" Paul yelled, pointing into the ocean.

Heading directly for their boat, with sharp fins slicing through the bloody water, were three great white sharks.

The blood-maddened sharks were charging the boat from opposite directions, churning the water like a ghastly whirlpool of death. The foam was dyed a horrifying red! Chris swung one of the oars at the sharks and Steve used the other. Paul tried desperately to start the motor.

"Hurry!" shrieked Steve. "We'll try to hold them off as long as we can!"

One of the sharks leaped halfway out of the

water, ripping away part of the wooden bow. Splinters of wood flew into Steve's face, and he leaped back. With each vicious attack, Steve stared into the hideous, empty eyes of the huge shark.

"Watch it!" Paul cried.

With a tremendous leap, an enraged shark caught Chris's oar in its mouth and snapped it in two like it was a toothpick!

"Dad! Hurry! I'm scared!" howled Chris.

Water sloshed over the sides, beginning to fill the bottom of the boat. Steve slammed his oar over one shark's back. But he lost his footing in the slippery, rocking boat and fell backward. He almost tipped the whole boat over. Chris pulled him into the center of the dinghy.

Finally, the boat motor sputtered to life and the rowboat jerked forward, knocking against the hull of the *Brittania* before sliding back into the bloody sea. Paul turned the leaking boat toward the nearest shore and opened the throttle all the way. It was a race against death!

The sharks continued to ram the boat, smashing against its flimsy wooden sides like living torpedoes. Each terrible blow caused more damage, cracking and splintering the wood, until seawater rushed into the bottom of the boat.

"Bail!" shouted Paul.

Chris used a plastic pail to shovel the water off the bottom of the boat and over the side.

"Faster!" cried Paul.

The sharks circled the boat ever more tightly, as if they sensed that their murderous hunt would soon be over. Their hideous, leering eyes stared up at the victims in the slowly sinking rowboat.

The only hope lay in making it to shore 300 yards away. But between them and the beach lurked the most ghastly evil of the ocean. If the boat went down, the boys knew they would have as little chance as the victims of the *Britannia* did long ago.

The water surged through the cracks in the wood. No matter how fast Chris bailed, the water seemed to get deeper and deeper. Each time a shark struck at the boat, more water came in through the cracks.

Slowly, the boat moved toward shore, a wake of bloody water trailing behind it.

"I don't think we're going to make it!" cried a hysterical Chris.

"Look!" Steve shouted. "In the water!"

As they all looked in stunned horror and amazement, two of the sharks attacked the other one. They tore it to pieces, hungrily ripping off chunks of flesh. The last they saw of the unlucky victim was its blank, staring eye as it fell away, mortally wounded, down into the depths of the ocean. The other two followed it down, attacking and ripping it apart to satisfy their appetites.

As quickly as the sharks had appeared, they were gone. The surface of the sea became smooth, with no hint of the terror except the pinkish color of the sea foam. The three in the boat collapsed in exhaustion and fear.

It wasn't until they were pulling the half-destroyed boat up onto the beach that anyone could speak.

"W-what happened, Dad? Why didn't they—"

"I'm not sure, Chris," Paul answered. "But I've read that sharks can be so maddened by the taste of blood that if an attacking shark is cut or injured, the others will turn on it and tear it to pieces. That must be what happened."

Chris shook his head. "I know as long as I live I'll never forget the eyes of those sharks."

Paul looked out at the sea that had almost been their grave. He said softly, "Those monsters will even eat each other to satisfy their thirst for blood!"

CHAPTER FIVE
The Riddle of the Medallion

T HE next morning, Paul left for another island to inspect a different wreck for the adventure tour. A few minutes after he left, Chris and Steve headed into town.

"Let's see if we can find anybody in the fishing village who knows what's happening on that ship," said Chris.

"You know the last thing your dad said was that we shouldn't go near that wreck."

"We're not going near the wreck," said Chris. "We're going to the village, that's all. I just want to have a look around."

"I guess your theory about it being Edward out on the wreck is shot," said Chris. "Dad said he denied everything. Edward told Dad he can't speak a word of Spanish."

Steve shook his head. "Boy, it sure sounded like him. But maybe your dad's right. What would Edward be doing out on that boat if he won't even take us out there?"

After walking into town, they rented two bicycles and set off pedaling for the small village they had seen from the boat the day before. They arrived in the village in the early afternoon. Small shacks stood along the docks on the edge of the sea. There were shops and cafes along the main street. Almost all the fishing boats were out at sea.

Chris and Steve leaned their bicycles against a soda machine. They wandered along the main street and paused at different shops, listening carefully to voices and studying the faces of the people they saw.

Most of the people were tourists, but they could tell that some were villagers. Almost everyone spoke English. In an outdoor cafe at the end of the street, they heard Spanish spoken. They went over to listen more closely. Two old men were sitting with a young woman at a table near the cafe entrance. They were speaking in low voices.

"It's not them," said Steve.

"Doesn't hurt to ask a few questions," said Chris. "Maybe they'll understand English."

They crossed the street and went up to the people at the table. Chris spoke to them in English and they answered. The people seemed friendly until Chris mentioned the

Britannia. Then, the woman cried, "Get away from me! That ship is evil," she said in English, spitting the words at him. "Anyone who goes near it deserves his fate!" She turned away and said nothing more.

The boys left the cafe and continued wandering through the streets of the village.

"Boy," said Steve. "You definitely said the wrong thing when you mentioned the wreck."

Chris nodded.

At every store or cafe, they stopped to listen. Sometimes they moved on quickly. Sometimes they asked about the wreck. But no one wanted to talk about it. Almost everyone seemed frightened and walked away as soon as the boys asked about the ship. Some spit on the ground to frighten away evil spirits. Others told them to go away and to have nothing to do with the shipwreck. One toothless old man laughed hysterically and told them that the cries of the trapped passengers and their blinking candles had made him crazy!

"I think everyone believes the story about the ghosts and the haunted wreck," said Steve after they had walked almost the whole length of the main street.

"Well, I don't know what's really going on," answered Chris. "But we know there's something out there—ghosts or not!"

"I don't think we're going to find out anything here," said Steve. "You want to head back to the hotel?"

"Not yet," said Chris, turning back to the docks. "Let's stay a little while longer. I just have a feeling that the clue we're looking for is here somewhere."

They strolled up and down the streets of the village until almost 5:00, when the fishing boats were beginning to return to port. Not a single person had been willing to talk to them about the *Britannia*. Disappointed, they had started back to their bikes when they saw a fishing boat backing into one of the docks.

A large, bald man with huge arms was leaning over the edge of the boat. He was loading boxes of fish onto the dock. A few other men were helping him. As the boys watched from across the road, one of the men let a box slip. It fell on the big man's foot, and he yelled loudly in Spanish. His voice wheezed and rasped.

"Chris! That voice! That's one of the guys we heard on the wreck," Steve said.

"Are you sure?" Chris asked.

"Yeah, come on!"

They left their bicycles and went across the street. They stood at the back of the crowd that had gathered to watch the argument.

The man's loud voice filled the street.

"I'm sure he's the one we heard inside the wreck!" said Steve. "What are we going to do?"

"I'll write down the name of the boat they're on. Then we can tell Dad. He'll know what to do."

"But your dad's still on that other island," said Steve.

"Let's get back to the hotel as fast as we can," said Chris, getting on his bike. "We can tell him as soon as he comes back."

They pedaled furiously back to St. George. By the time they returned the bicycles to the shop and reached their hotel, Mrs. Marlow was setting the table for dinner.

"Well, boys, I almost gave you up for lost," she said. "Your father's not here yet."

The boys went up to their room to talk about what they should do. "Maybe that fisherman guy can lead us to the others," said Chris.

"Do you think we should call the police?"

"Let's tell Dad first," said Chris. "He can help us decide what to do."

But Paul hadn't arrived by 7:00, and Mrs. Marlow went ahead and served dinner. After they had eaten, Chris and Steve waited on the front porch for Paul to come home. The sun was low in the western sky. Neither boy said much as they rocked nervously in the creaky old rocking chairs.

"Where do you think he is?" asked Steve, after they had been waiting almost 45 minutes. "Do you think something's happened?"

"I don't know. Maybe he stopped off at Edward's store," said Chris. "It's open late tonight."

"Do you think so?"

"Well, maybe he tried to get him to lead the trip one more time."

Steve chewed his fingernails.

"Do those taste good?" Chris asked. "Are they better than nice, sweet rockfish?"

"Shut up, I can't help it. I just wish your dad would hurry up and get home."

"Well, I'm sick of sitting here doing nothing," said Chris, jumping up. "Let's go over to Edward's store."

"I don't know. Maybe we ought to wait here for your dad."

"Sometimes you're such a chicken," said Chris.

"I'm not a chicken," said Steve, "I'm just careful. This might be dangerous stuff, especially if that was Edward on the wreck. He might be mixed up in the whole thing."

"What's the worst that can happen?" asked Chris. "We'll come back here without Dad, right?"

Steve thought for a moment, then answered, "Yeah, I guess so."

"Come on, then."

The alleys and streets were dark as they made their way down the road toward Edward's scuba shop. When they reached the shop, its shutters were drawn closed.

"It looks like we made the trip for nothing," said Steve, turning around. "His house is dark, too."

Chris grabbed his arm and led him toward the door. They stopped on the front porch.

"Wait a minute. Something's funny," he said, shaking his head.

"What?" asked Steve.

"There's something crunching under our shoes. Don't move!" whispered Chris.

"What is it?"

Chris peered into the darkness at his feet. Something glittered in the faint light. "Glass!" he said.

Jagged pieces of broken glass lay scattered on the ground.

"Look at the door!" cried Steve.

In the dim light Chris saw a hole the size of a fist above the door's lock. Someone had smashed in the window! Chris pushed the door slightly. It swung open.

"Be careful," Steve whispered. "There could still be someone in there."

Carefully, Chris and Steve stepped over the

broken glass. They listened for sounds of someone still in the shop. It was deathly quiet.

"Where's the light?" asked Steve.

"Try the wall near the door," said Chris.

Steve flipped on the light switch.

"Oh, no! It looks like a hurricane's been through here," said Chris.

They looked around the room in amazement. Broken diving masks and fish tanks were strewn about. Rubber flippers, T-shirts, and sandals lay in piles. The cash register had been thrown on its side under the counter. Racks with books and magazines had been turned over. Fishing tackle and fish hooks were tangled on the floor. But there was no one in the shop.

"Edward's been robbed!" cried Chris.

"No, I don't think so," said Steve, kneeling by the cash register. "Whoever came here wanted something besides money. The cash register hasn't been opened!"

"What does it mean?" asked Chris.

"Let's just keep searching," said Steve.

They rummaged through the mess for another 10 minutes. Steve crawled on the floor looking for clues, while Chris went into the back room. Finally, Steve stood up.

"We'd better call the police," he said.

"I guess so," said Chris. "Wait!"

"What?"

"It might get Edward in trouble," Chris said.

"Hey, look around!" Steve answered. "Edward's already in trouble!"

"But he is Dad's old friend. Maybe we should talk to Dad about it first."

"Well, maybe you're right," Steve answered after a second. "What do we do, then?"

"Let me think. Let's look around more."

Steve went and searched near the books and magazines. Chris rummaged through some of the boxes. He lifted up a box and was about to put it down when he saw something on the floor gleam in the light.

"Hey, Steve, come over here!" he cried.

"What?"

"Look at this," said Chris. "I found it by the counter."

"That's Edward's good luck medallion from the ship!" said Steve.

They gazed at the small, shiny piece of metal, with the word *Brittania* engraved on the front. There were reddish streaks across the face of the medallion.

"Is that blood?" asked Steve.

Chris nodded his head. "If it's Edward's blood, that means he's been hurt," said Chris.

The boys stared at each other and then around at the ransacked shop. "I think somebody took him away," said Steve.

"There was definitely a struggle here," said Chris. "And he must have fought back."

"It must mean something!" Steve muttered, smashing his fist down. "We've got clues. We just have to know how to read them."

He picked up a chair that had been turned upside down and sat in it. Chris leaned against the counter with folded arms.

"Okay. let's say somebody did kidnap him," Steve began. "Why?"

"Because he's mixed up somehow in the stuff on the ghost ship."

"That's it!" Steve yelled, standing up. "That has to be it. And this good luck charm is a clue. Edward said he never went anywhere without the medallion. He must have left it behind as a clue to where they were taking him!"

"I see what you mean! Where's the one place that they could hide him?"

"Somewhere deserted."

"A place nobody could reach."

They both stood staring down at the piece of metal in Chris's hand. The letters stood out in the dim light.

"The *Brittania!*" they cried together.

"Come on, let's go," said Chris, shoving the medallion into his pocket. "We've got to find Dad and get out to the wreck! We might not have much time to save Edward!"

CHAPTER SIX
Voices in the Night

CHRIS and Steve raced back to Mrs. Marlow's. Their faces fell when she told them that Paul still hadn't returned. They looked at each other grimly. They knew what they had to do.

Chris took a piece of paper from the desk in the lobby. *Dad,* he wrote, *come out to the wreck as fast as you can! Edward's in danger!*

Chris folded the letter and gave it to Mrs. Marlow.

"Is anything wrong?" she asked.

"Make sure my dad gets the message. It's a matter of life and death!" Chris shouted, dashing out the door with Steve behind him.

They sprinted down the dark trail along the beach to Somer's Wharf. The shops in town were closed and the streets were empty. The shades in the windows of the boat rental shop were drawn. At the end of the dock Chris spotted a dinghy. He ran the length of the dock and leaped into the boat. Steve untied the rope from the wooden railing and jumped in after him.

"Is there any gas?" asked Steve.

"We'll know in a minute."

The boat drifted slowly away from the pier. Twice, Chris pulled hard on the cord. Nothing happened. Once more Chris yanked on the cord and this time the engine caught. It lurched forward, sending the boys flying.

"Look out!" cried Steve.

The boat veered straight for the dock. Grabbing the rudder just in time, Chris steered the boat away from the dock toward the open harbor. When Chris opened the throttle, the boat shuddered and sped over the pitch-black sea toward the *Britannia*.

There was just enough light from the stars for them to find their way. The moon hadn't risen yet. Islands loomed like murky shadows to their right. Both boys scanned the smooth water for the dreaded white fins.

They cruised at top speed for 20 minutes. Ahead of them a few hundred yards, the wreck of the *Britannia* loomed. They could see faint yellow lights in a few of the portholes.

"Kill the engine," said Steve.

Chris pushed in the choke, and the engine made a soft, sputtering sound. Then there was silence. All they could hear were waves slapping against the sides of the dinghy.

Using the oars to stay on course, Chris let the boat drift toward the wreck. Without any moon, they were cloaked in darkness. In another hour, when the moon began to rise, they knew it would be different. For now, though, they were almost invisible, as long as they made no sound.

The eerie yellow light from the wreck shimmered on the sea's surface and flickered on and off underwater. It was easy to see why people on the island thought that the shimmering light looked like the candles of the drowned passengers.

Suddenly in the dim light, Steve recognized the triangular shape of a shark's fin slicing through the water between them and the wreck.

He motioned toward the shark.

"I think there's only one," whispered Chris. "Maybe it'll leave us alone. Keep this handy," he added, handing one of the oars to Steve. He used the other to paddle closer to the wreck.

The shark circled closer, its fin cutting the water less than 20 yards from their boat. Steve lifted the oar, ready to strike.

"Do you hear any noise coming from the wreck?" Chris asked in a whisper.

"No," said Steve, not taking his eyes off the circling shark. Just as suddenly as it appeared, the shark vanished.

Soon they pulled silently alongside the wreck. "Listen!" hissed Steve.

Inside the cabin, they heard a jumble of voices, excited and angry. They recognized the wheeze of the fat man they had seen on the dock in the fishing village.

"That's him again!" said Steve.

"Keep the boat from hitting the hull!" whispered Chris.

Quickly, Steve stood up in the bow of the boat. Resting his hands against the hull, he held the boat away from the hull so that it wouldn't knock against it. The hull was like a big echo chamber. Any sound at all would alert the people inside.

Steve looked down into the sea. With a gasp, he saw that the single shark had returned, joined by several others. Beneath the surface he could see their sleek bodies gliding dangerously near the boat, waiting.

He tried not to look down.

Inside the cabin the talking ceased. Someone moaned.

"What was that?" asked Chris.

They heard it again—a low, weak voice, in pain.

Right above them was a rusted hook of some kind. Chris reached up and tied the dinghy's rope to the hook to keep the boat from drifting away. As he stepped up onto the deck of the wreck, his foot slipped on some seaweed and he slid out over the water. His shoulders fell against the ship's hull with a dull thud. For a dreadful instant, Chris was suspended a few feet above the water, where the sharks glided and waited.

But he managed to grab the rusty hook. Chris froze. If anyone had heard the sound and came out and looked over the side, they'd see him right away.

Don't let go, don't let go, he silently repeated to himself.

For what seemed like an eternity, he hung there on the side, a few feet above the powerful jaws and daggerlike teeth of the sharks. Finally, when his arms seemed about to be pulled out of their sockets, he started to haul himself up. Searching for a foothold on the side of the rusting hull, Chris inched slowly up the side of the wreck.

From below Steve watched him, not daring to breathe. But Chris made it over the upper deck's railing and disappeared. He came back a few moments later and threw a rope he had found down to Steve. Steve tied it around his waist and started climbing up the side of the hull. He too kept his eyes up, not daring to look down into the sea.

When they were both safely on deck, Chris whispered, "I don't think anybody heard me."

They crept silently to the other side of the wreck, the side that was hidden from shore. Less than 30 yards away, a large speedboat sat in the water. They could just make out the profile of a man kneeling in the stern. He was cradling a rifle in his arms.

"Since when do ghosts carry guns?" asked Steve.

"Or drive speedboats?" asked Chris.

In the darkness, they knew they were nearly invisible, as long as they stayed on their hands and knees. They crawled across the hull until they heard the voices directly beneath them.

"Can you understand what they're saying?"

"No, they're speaking Spanish too fast," said Steve.

Chris lowered himself over the side of the hull to look in the porthole. For a moment he almost lost his grip. His foot scuffed against the rusting ship's side as he tried regain his balance. The scraping sound seemed to echo in the stillness.

The boys froze. Their hearts almost stopped when they heard a metal door slam and footsteps heading their way.

"Quick," whispered Chris. "Over the side."

"What about the sharks?"

"We don't have any choice," said Chris, scrambling down the side of the hull and lowering himself toward the water. Steve followed. Together they hung against the side, only a foot or so out of the water.

Above them they heard footsteps scraping against the deck. Steve pulled his knees under his chin, trying to keep as far out of the water as possible. The footsteps stopped directly over them.

Two men talked in Spanish and laughed. One of them tossed a cigarette into the water near Steve's foot. The boys stayed as still as they could. Both imagined the shark attack that might come at any second. If they cried out, the men would find them.

But it would be even worse if the attack came so suddenly they didn't even have time to scream.

"Que pasa, amigo?" said one of the men on deck to another. They stood and looked out at the ocean.

"Don't move," mouthed Chris.

Finally the two men strolled away toward the front of the ship. As their footsteps grew fainter, Chris let out a silent sigh of relief.

Moving slightly to his left, Steve felt something hard bump against his leg. He began to cry out, but stifled his scream. He almost fainted with fear, imagining the razor-sharp teeth tearing into his body.

But Steve saw that the surface of the water near him was smooth. He turned his head to find that he had bumped against a filthy canvas bag, hanging by a rope in the water next to him.

The bag was stained with blood.

He pulled himself out of the water as quickly as he could. Chris followed. "W-what the—" Steve whispered when the footsteps had finally died away.

Steve reached over the side and touched the bag. It felt wet and sticky. When he pulled his hand away, it was covered with blood.

"It feels horrible," he said, wiping his hand on his shirt. Together, they loosened the rope around the top of the bag. There was a horrible stench. Holding their breath, they looked inside.

Chris gagged at the hideous sight inside the bag. "It's filled with dead animals! Why would anyone do this?"

"I know why," said Steve softly. "Because someone wants the sharks here."

"Yeah," answered his cousin. "It's starting to

make sense now. The sharks, the stories about the ghosts . . . "

"But what are those men doing in the wreck and what does Edward have to do with it?"

"That's what we have to find out," Chris answered grimly.

Just then, from the open porthole where they had heard the voices before, they heard a horrible scream and a cry of pain.

"I know that voice!" whispered Chris, grabbing his cousin's arm.

Steve nodded. "There's no doubt about it this time," he answered.

CHAPTER SEVEN
Race Against Death

BECAUSE of the way the wreck was tilting on the reef, the boys could just reach the lighted porthole where they had heard the voices. Luckily, there was a ledge that they could stand on. Chris stepped up and carefully peeped in. Steve joined him.

They saw six men gathered in a circle around another man who was tied to a chair. The backs of the six men were toward Chris and Steve. The small room was filled with smoke from the cigarettes that the men were smoking. They noticed that each man had a gun.

"They've got Edward," Chris whispered.

One of the men stood over Edward, his legs planted widely apart and his powerful arms hanging at his sides. He spoke angrily in Spanish. Then he raised his arm and struck Edward.

Edward groaned, and his head fell forward.

Chris and Steve watched one of the men go out of the room. When he came back, he was carrying a bucket. He handed the bucket to the large man, who emptied the bucket over Edward's head. All the men laughed loud, cruel laughs.

The man who had hit Edward turned around to talk to another man. It was the man with the raspy voice! Chris and Steve ducked beneath the porthole, out of sight. Then they carefully lifted their heads to look through the porthole again. They saw the leader holding a small alarm clock attached to a brown box the size of a small package.

Edward's eyes flickered open. Holding his fist in front of Edward's face, the man opened three fingers, one at a time, counting in Spanish.

"What's he saying?" asked Chris.

"Something about 15 minutes," said Steve.

"What about 15 minutes?" Chris asked.

Steve didn't say anything, but Chris quickly got his answer.

The large man kneeled in front of Edward. His hands were resting on his chest. Without warning he jumped into the air, his hands stretched toward the ceiling.

"Boom!!" he yelled, laughing like a fiend.

The other men all laughed, too. Then the boss threw the package across the room to one of the men, and they emptied quickly out of the cabin.

"They're going to blow the boat to pieces!" said Chris.

"In 15 minutes!" added Steve, glancing at his watch.

"With Edward tied to that chair!"

"Listen!" said Steve. "The men are coming up!"

"We'll have to go back over the side to hide from them," Chris whispered.

"But the sharks . . . "

"Come on!"

Chris struggled down the side of the hull. He hung just above the waterline. Steve cautiously followed him. Just below them, the sea washed against the bag of dead animals. Huddling next to each other, they waited until they couldn't hear the voices anymore.

"Do you think they're gone?" asked Steve.

"Let's take a look."

One after the other, they climbed back up the side of the hull toward the cabin. The ship seemed to be empty.

They slipped into the cabin where the men had been. Edward was bleary-eyed and bleeding from the beating. He didn't seem to recognize them and groaned when they approached his chair.

"Edward! Don't worry! It's us, Chris and Steve."

The boys looked with horror at the poor man's face. It was bruised from the punches he had taken. One eye was swollen shut.

Steve pulled at the ropes that pinned Edward's hands behind him. Chris knelt to untie the knots around his ankles. Edward tried to say something. But the boys couldn't understand him.

"We'll be off this wreck in a few minutes," said Chris. "Our boat is tied right outside."

"We found your good luck medallion," Steve explained. "We knew you'd never go anywhere without it. So we figured it had to be a clue."

Edward nodded.

From the back of the wreck, they heard laughing.

"*Adios, amigo,*" shouted one of the men.

"No, no," cried another one, "*adios, amigos!*"

There was another fit of laughter before the speedboat's engine started up. Steve went to the porthole. He watched the boat's powerful motors churn the dark water into a white foam. He saw the boat speed away.

"I wonder what was so funny. Are they gone?" asked Chris.

"It looks like it," Steve said, returning to Edward. "Don't worry," he said to Edward.

"Everything's going to be okay."

"Can you walk?" asked Chris.

"I need help," Edward groaned.

With his arms over their shoulders, they half-carried, half-dragged Edward out of the cabin. They squeezed down the narrow corridor.

"How do we get out of here?" asked Chris, searching the cramped hallway for an exit.

"This way," mumbled Edward, motioning with his head to a door on their right. "To the upper deck."

The stairway was too narrow for both boys to carry him. Chris went first, holding Edward under the arms. Steve carried Edward's feet.

"Faster! We don't have much time!" Chris yelled, glancing at his watch.

After helping Edward crawl through the narrow doorway, they carried him across the deck and hoisted him over the side of the hull.

"The boat's right here, Edward," said Steve. "Don't worry."

Steve lowered Edward carefully onto Chris's shoulder. Chris creeped down to the waterline, ready to lower Edward into the dinghy.

"Hey, I thought we left the boat here," said Chris.

"Yeah, this is the place," answered Steve.

"It—it's not here!" Chris cried.

"What do you mean?!"

"The boat's gone!" Chris wailed. "We're trapped!"

"But we tied it to that hook right down there!" shouted Steve.

"There it is!" said Edward. He pointed at the dark outline of their boat about 50 yards out to sea. And between them and their boat they saw the ghostly white fins of half a dozen sharks!

"But how could it have come loose?" Chris screamed. "I tied it with four knots!"

Steve reached over the edge down to the rusty hook. "Here's the answer," he said, holding up the end of the boat rope.

"Oh, no!" Chris said. "It's been cut!"

Steve stared at the neatly cut end of the rope that had held their escape. "That second guy who yelled 'Adios, amigos'?"

"Yeah?"

"Now I know what he meant," explained Steve. "He knew we were on the boat. And he knew we were planning to escape in the rowboat."

Chris caught Steve's eye. "Cutting that rope was our death sentence!" he said.

They stood together, staring across the water at the drifting rowboat, their only hope of escape. Suddenly, a sound made them look down below them.

What they had heard was the sickening thud of a shark hitting the bag of dead animals. The creature ripped into the bag and tore out a chunk. It sank below the moonlit surface as blood from the bag slowly spread across the dark water.

"We wouldn't have a chance if we swam for the boat," said Steve softly. "No chance at all."

"We've got to find that bomb and disconnect it!" cried Chris. He looked at his watch and said, "We don't have much time."

"They set the timer for 15 minutes," said Edward as he lifted himself up. "There's not more than 10 minutes left. You go look for the bomb. I'll be okay."

"Let's go!" shouted Chris.

They scampered over the side of the hull to the upper deck. Racing back to the cabin, they sprinted through the empty corridors, scanning the floor and walls for a sign of the bomb.

"See anything?" shouted Steve. He had dropped to his knees in the hallway outside the cabin where the men had been holding Edward. Finding nothing, he went into the cabin across the hall, searching the floor and the corners of the room for some clue.

"Nothing yet," shouted Chris from another cabin further down the hall.

"How much time is left?" Steve called.

"Maybe eight minutes."

"I don't see it! We'll never find it!"

"Keep looking!" cried Chris.

Steve raced down the corridor and looked in rooms further down the hall. In one of the rooms he found some old cabinets. He tore open each one, throwing the junk out on the floor.

Chris was looking outside the cabin.

"Find anything?" called Steve.

"Nothing!"

"How much time?"

Chris checked his watch.

"Six minutes!" he yelled.

They spent another few minutes frantically searching through old musty cabins and hallways. Deep inside the dark wreck it was almost impossible to see. With a growing sense of panic and desperation, the boys became more and more frightened.

"Five minutes!" screamed Chris.

They heard Edward crying out weakly from the side the hull. "Hurry! The water's rising!"

"I think it's all over," said Steve when they met out on the deck. "That bomb could be anywhere on this whole ship. We'd never find it if we looked for a month!"

Chris stared at his cousin. "Come on," he said grimly. "Let's go get Edward. We're going to have to swim for it."

They leaped over the railing and slid down the side of the slanting hull. There they saw Edward lying on his back, half-conscious. The water lapped at his feet, washing over his ankles.

Less than 10 feet away were four sharks. Their white fins gleamed in the moonlight, and their hideous eyes looked like the eyes of dead men.

"Edward's too weak to swim," said Steve.

"You're right," he said, looking around. "I know what we can do," he added, grabbing a loose piece of the white wooden railing.

"Here, Edward," Chris said, kneeling next to the man. "We're going to try to swim for the rowboat. We'll help you hold on to this. It'll keep you afloat."

Edward nodded slowly, then moaned. His eyes were now swollen completely shut.

"Help me hold him," said Chris.

They moved Edward to the edge of the dark water and were about to slip him in. Suddenly Chris cried out. "The sharks are coming!"

One of the sharks swept in front of Chris and slashed the canvas bag that hung in the water. It tore off a chunk of dead meat, spreading more blood over the surface of the water.

"Here come two more," cried Steve. "Help me pull Edward back!"

Two more sharks swam swiftly past Chris, tearing at the rest of the bag with their gruesome jaws. The boys pulled the now-blind Edward out of the water as far as they could.

"That's what they'll do to us if they get the chance!" shouted Chris.

"Untie that bag!" yelled Steve. "If it sinks, maybe it'll draw the sharks away long enough for us to swim to the boat!"

Chris began madly clawing at the knots that fastened the bag of dead animals to the side of the ship. "It's too tight!" he screamed. "I can't get it loose!"

"We've got to get it loose!" Steve howled in desperation and terror as he tried to help Chris with the knots. "We've only got a few seconds left!"

CHAPTER EIGHT
It's All Over!

WHICH would it be: the sharks or the bomb? They gave up trying to untie the knot. Less than five feet from where Steve, Chris, and Edward huddled in fear, the sharks were ripping the canvas bag to shreds. They churned the water into a foam of ghastly pink.

But somewhere deep inside the wreck, a bomb timer was ticking away their last few moments on earth. And they could do nothing to stop it!

Their eyes met as they moved closer together. "I can't do it!" cried Chris. "I can't go into the water with those monsters! It would be too terrible!"

Steve was too scared to answer. He only nodded. Both boys were trembling so badly they could barely hold on to the ledge that kept them from sliding into the bloody water. Edward lay moaning, blind and semi-conscious.

Together they waited helplessly for the end they knew was near.

"Wait!" Steve suddenly screamed. "Do you hear that?"

"What?"

"Listen!"

From over the water came a strange buzzing sound. The boys thought for a moment that they were imagining it. But the sound was becoming louder with each passing second.

"Where is it?" yelled Steve, searching the darkness.

"Is it a boat?" screamed Chris. "Maybe they're coming back to finish us off!"

"Do you hear something?" Edward asked weakly.

"There it is again," said Steve.

"It's coming closer."

"Look!" Steve screamed. "There it is! Up in the sky! It's a helicopter!"

Suddenly the sound changed to a high-pitched whine. It was so loud it sounded as if it was almost on top of them. Above them in the darkness was a blur of spinning blades and lights blinking on and off. Large, white letters spelled P-O-L-I-C-E.

"I don't believe it," said Steve.

"Believe it," said Chris.

Hovering over the wreck, the chopper

dropped down another 10 feet. The sound was incredibly loud. In the darkness something white fluttered into the air just a few feet above their heads. It was a sling attached to a rope. Chris jumped to grab it, but it swung out of his reach.

"Hurry up!" yelled Steve.

"It's too high."

Holding on to Edward with one arm, Steve used the other arm to motion the pilot to bring the helicopter in closer. The sling swung back and forth, just barely out of their reach.

"What are you waiting for?" cried Steve.

"Help me grab hold of it!"

After three tries, Chris managed to jump onto it. It spun crazily away from the wreck, making him dizzy. But he managed to climb the rope ladder one foot at a time. Turning toward the boat, he reached down for Edward.

"Hurry it up!" shouted Steve above the noise of the chopper blades. "The ship's going to blow any second!"

Steve lifted Edward up to Chris.

Wrapping an arm around one of the ropes, Edward held on tightly as Chris pulled him up.

Only Steve remained behind on the wreck.

"Jump!" cried Chris, as the helicopter lifted a few feet higher.

"I'll never make it!" yelled Steve.

"You've got to try!"

Just then the sling swung back toward the wreck.

"Now!" shouted Chris. *Or never,* he added to himself.

Steve leaped across open space for the sling, grabbing wildly. His desperate fingers closed around the rope and his foot reached for the sling. He was safe.

But the added weight of a third person on the sling pulled it down several feet. It swung out away from the wreck over the bloody, churning water. For one endless, horrifying moment, Steve dangled only inches above the blood-crazed killers of the ocean. He felt the splash of the bloody water. He was close enough to stare into the unspeakably hideous eyes of death.

Then the helicopter started to lift slowly and Steve rose from the water. As soon as they had cleared the wreck, Chris signaled to the pilot to pull them up. But they were still not out of danger.

Tilting away from the sea, the helicopter rose quickly, picking up speed. The warm air rushed past them and they tightened their grips on the rope. Suddenly without warning, a huge explosion ripped the night air. Gigantic sprays of water filled the sky around them.

Below, flames shot out of the ship's cabin and raced across the water. Then another explosion, even louder than the first, roared below them. Bright yellow and red streaks of flame clawed the air, bathing the sea in a frightening, fiery glow.

Steve imagined what had happened to the sharks caught in the explosion. He didn't feel one bit sorry for them.

The helicopter was heading for the shore. Its engines were so loud that the three of them couldn't talk. But Chris gave the thumbs up, and Steve patted Edward on the shoulder. They felt the rope sling slowly rising toward the chopper. Little by little, the rope was hauled in, and they inched toward the helicopter's open door.

Finally, an arm reached out of the door, and a hand grabbed the sling. Chris reached for the hand and dove into the cabin of the helicopter. Looking around him, he laughed with relief. It was his father's hand.

In another instant, Steve and Edward were safe inside and the helicopter was moving toward land at full speed. It flew to the island and 10 minutes later, they were met by a police car and a doctor at the airport. Their ordeal was over.

* * * * *

Less than an hour later, they were all in the lobby of Mrs. Marlow's hotel. The doctor had said Edward would be all right with rest. He slumped in a chair, explaining everything to the local police chief, Inspector Barrett.

"So, you see," said Edward, his voice still shaking, "they kidnapped my son and forced me to help them." Ice packs had reduced some of the swelling on his eyes and face.

"Who were they?" asked Inspector Barrett.

"Columbian drug smugglers," said Edward, leaning back and sipping tea out of the cup that Mrs. Marlow had brought him. "They used Bermuda as their base for shipping cocaine into the U.S. every month."

Inspector Barrett whistled softly. "Where is your son now?" he asked.

Edward's eyes widened and filled with tears. He held his head in his hands.

"Oh, Anthony, my son," he moaned, rocking back and forth in his chair. "I don't know where he is. They may still have him." Edward's sobs were heartbreaking to hear.

Paul walked over to Edward and put his arm around him. "I'm sure Anthony will be all right," he said. "There would be no reason for the smugglers to hurt him."

Edward stopped sobbing after a while and he looked up.

"So that was why you wanted us to try another ship," said Paul. "You were hoping that we'd leave the smugglers alone?"

"That's right," said Edward. "They would have killed my son. They told me to make sure that no one ever got near that ship."

"But how did you meet them?" asked Steve.

"They came to me to find out about diving equipment and places to dive," Edward explained. "I thought they were tourists. But I was wrong. They were looking for a place to run their drug smuggling ring from."

"So they blackmailed you," said the inspector. "Saying they would hurt your son."

Edward nodded. "They made me spread stories about the ghosts to keep people away from the ship. What could I do? To save my son's life, I would have done almost anything."

The police inspector nodded and wrote in his notebook.

"Spreading the stories was easy," Edward continued. "Everyone knows the strange stories about the mysterious Bermuda Triangle and how the ships disappear. Whenever I passed through the village, I told someone else another awful story about the ship. I told them the lights were the candles of the drowned passengers. It's easy for people to believe evil things."

"But the lights were really the drug smugglers!" said Steve.

"Right," Edward replied. "And the sounds and voices—they were all the smugglers."

"You did a good job of scaring the people," said Chris. "When we were asking around about the ship, nobody would talk to us at all!"

Edward nodded grimly. "That wasn't all me scaring them. I feel terrible about those two divers who were killed."

"So you think it was the drug smugglers who killed them?" the police chief asked.

"No doubt about it. They got too close to the *Britannia*," explained Edward. "They paid with their lives."

"What else did you do to help them?" asked Inspector Barrett.

Edward explained how the smugglers used a fishing boat, the one that Chris and Steve had seen in the harbor unloading, to get the cocaine back to land. Edward was forced to give them diving equipment.

"Why were the smugglers beating you up?" asked Inspector Barrett.

"They thought I had betrayed them," said Edward. "When the two boys started looking around and asking questions, the smugglers thought I had told them about the operation."

"And that was you we heard on the boat?" asked Steve.

Edward nodded.

"You can speak Spanish!" Steve declared.

"Si, amigo."

"And what's this Chris was telling me about your good luck piece?" asked Paul.

Chris took the medallion from his pocket and handed it back to Edward.

"Ah, my good luck piece," he said, holding it tightly in his hand. "I was hoping that someone would find it."

"You left it as a clue, right?" asked Steve.

"That's right," answered Edward. "When the smugglers came to get me in my shop, they tried to make it look like a robbery. But before they dragged me away, I dropped my good luck medallion on the floor, hoping someone would find it and know where I was."

"We were lucky to find it," said Steve.

"It was more than luck, boys," said Inspector Barrett, smiling. "It was a very good piece of detective work."

Chris and Steve found themselves blushing at the police chief's praise.

"What about the sharks?" asked Chris.

"Well, the smugglers figured sharks would

keep people away," said Edward. "Sharks, and the legends about the haunted ship and the Bermuda Triangle. They hung the bag of dead animals over the side of the boat to attract those horrible creatures."

Steve shivered, remembering how near he came to being eaten alive by the sharks.

"How did you know where to come find us?" asked Edward.

"The boys left a message with Mrs. Marlow," said Paul. "I called the police."

"And I ordered the helicopter as soon as he called," said Inspector Barrett. "Another minute and I'm afraid we would have been too late."

Just then a young policeman burst into the room. He saluted when he saw Inspector Barrett.

"Yes, Sergeant?" asked Inspector Barrett.

"Two things to report, Sir."

"Yes?"

"We have captured the smugglers and their speedboat, Sir," explained the sergeant. "They are now behind bars in St. George, Sir."

"Excellent!" cried the inspector. "What is the other thing you have to report?"

"Sir, the boy is safe."

"Anthony? My son is safe?" cried Edward, lowering his head into his hands and sobbing. "Oh, thank heavens! He's safe!"

"He was being held in a warehouse outside the village," said the sergeant. "They had tied him to a chair. He was able to escape when the smugglers left to go out to the wreck."

"Well," said Inspector Barrett, turning toward Edward, "it looks like everything will be—"

At that moment, a boy with short curly hair and bright, dark eyes burst into the hotel's lobby. Sobbing, he rushed into Edward's arms.

"Poppa," he wailed.

"It's all right, Anthony," whispered Edward, stroking the back of his son's head, his own eyes shut tightly against tears. "It's all over, son. It's all over."

CHAPTER NINE
Homeward Bound

THE next night they were in the lobby of the hotel—Chris and Steve, Paul, Edward and his wife and son, Inspector Barrett, and Mrs. Marlow. They were waiting for the taxi to take Chris, Steve, and Paul to the airport.

It was warm, even with the ceiling fans spinning overhead. Mrs. Marlow disappeared into the kitchen and returned holding a small package wrapped in aluminum foil. She handed it to Chris.

"Here are a few more johnnycakes," she said, "for the plane ride home."

The boys laughed. "Uh, thanks, Mrs. Marlow," said Chris, stuffing the package into his backpack. "These will come in handy if we get hungry."

Outside a car horn honked loudly.

"Come on, guys," said Paul, "the taxi's waiting."

As they were walking outside, Steve

whispered to Chris, "I couldn't eat another johnnycake if you paid me."

"No kidding," answered Chris. "The only time they would have come in handy was when we needed something to plug the hole in the rowboat!"

Everyone moved outside onto the porch. It was the same taxi, the yellow Mercedes, that they had taken from the airport to Mrs. Marlow's less than a week ago. And the same driver stood behind the car unlocking the trunk.

"Here we go," said Edward, handing Paul's bag to the driver.

"Good-bye, Edward," said Paul.

"My friend, how can I thank you?" asked Edward, embracing Paul.

"You might think about leading another tour," said Paul, laughing.

Edward tilted his head back, flashing two rows of even, white teeth, and laughed. "Yes, yes, Just let me get back to normal," he replied. "I want to enjoy having Anthony back, safe and sound. I'll call you in a few weeks."

Then he turned to Chris and Steve. "It is you two that I owe everything to," he said. "I know I can never repay you for saving my life. I will never forget you. You are very brave men."

He shook hands with Chris and Steve and then hugged them. The boys smiled.

Then Anthony shyly stepped forward and shook hands, just like his father did. "Thank you," he said softly. "I hope you come back to Bermuda."

After a few more good-byes and thank-yous, Chris and Steve slid into the backseat. Paul slipped in next to them, pulling the door shut behind him.

"Okay, let's go," he said to the driver.

"Good-bye!" cried Mrs. Marlow.

"How did you enjoy your stay on our island?" asked the driver, after they had been driving for a few minutes.

"It's a very relaxing place," said Paul, winking at Chris and Steve.

"Yeah, we really liked the peace and quiet," said Steve. Chris nudged him in the ribs.

"Did you hear about the drug smugglers?" asked the driver.

"Uh, no," Paul answered with a smile. "What happened?"

"Well," said the driver, "some Columbian drug smugglers were using a sunken ship as a hide-out. I heard that some really tough Americans came down and broke up the whole drug ring and helped the police catch all the smugglers. Somebody told me that the Columbians were lucky to escape with their lives."

"Is that so?" asked Paul, trying to hide his

grin. "Sounds exciting."

Chris and Steve's stomachs began to hurt from trying not to laugh. When they reached the airport, the taxi pulled up to the curb to let them off. They hurried toward the gate.

"Watch out, everybody!" jabbered Chris as they hurried toward the departure gate. "Here come some really tough Americans!"

"Yeah," joked Steve, "I'm Sylvester Stallone and this is my buddy, Clint Eastwood. Pay us in johnnycakes and we'll break up drug smuggling rings!"

"Knock it off, guys," said Paul with a laugh. The boys doubled over with laughter.

They boarded their plane and got ready for takeoff. They could see the blue lights of the runway stretching into the distance.

"Well, it looks like we won't be taking a tour of the haunted ship," said Paul.

"Yeah," said Chris. "Since it exploded sky high, there's nothing left of it."

"So, that's the end of the Halloween trip?" asked Steve.

The plane leveled off. The stars shone brightly in the dark night sky.

"Not exactly," said Paul. "There's another wreck on a reef about a half-mile off the shore of Cobbler's Island. It's an old Spanish galleon that crashed on the reef centuries ago. Half of it is buried under sand. But there's enough of a ship left for people to explore. There might even be some treasure there."

"Ooh, that sounds cool!" said Steve. "And I bet all the publicity from the *Britannia* will help attract people."

"Sure," said his father. "It can't hurt."

"What about Edward?" asked Chris. "Will he lead the tour?"

"I've asked him to help," said Paul, "and I think he will. Right now, he's just happy to have his son back alive. After the great job he did making people believe there were ghosts on the *Britannia,* I'd like him to help us spread the word that this other ship is haunted, too."

"Will the police put him in jail?" asked Steve.

"No," said Paul, shaking his head. "I don't think so."

"Wasn't he helping the smugglers?" asked Steve.

"Yes, but they forced him. Now he's helping the police prosecute them."

Chris had been quiet for a few minutes, just staring out the window. "Hey, Dad?" he asked in a strange voice.

"Yeah?"

"Isn't that about where the *Britannia* was? Right down there?"

Paul glanced out the window. "That's right," he answered. "That's the island of St. David's."

"Well, if the ship sank out of sight," asked Chris, "w-what are those lights down there?"

"What?!"

Paul and Steve both leaned over Chris to look out the window. Right below them they saw the unmistakable shape of the haunted ship, just as it had been before the explosion. And dancing on the ship were hundreds of tiny lights about the size of candle flames.

"No!" cried Paul. "It's not possible!"

"H-how could the wreck come up to the surface again?" asked Steve. "We saw the whole thing disappear under the sea!"

"And what are those lights?" Chris cried in wonder and disbelief. "Dad, do you think? . . . Could they be? . . . "

Paul rubbed his eyes. "I just don't know, son. I can't believe it! There's definitely something down there," he said softly. "But what? There's got to be an explanation."

Paul shook his head. "It might be moonlight, or it might be small fish that glow or—or—"

Chris finished his sentence for him, as the plane banked away to the left and they lost sight of the eerie twinkling lights.

"—or it might be the candles of the drowned passengers, still trapped beneath the sea."

Check out *Shadow Over Loch Ness,* as Steve and Chris search for the terrifying secret hidden in the murky waters of Loch Ness!